THE GIRL IN THE
GOLDEN  BOWER

Written by

Illustrated by

JANE YOLEN   JANE DYER

For Elizabeth —
Enjoy the Magic!
Jane Dyer
1999

Little, Brown and Company
Boston New York Toronto London

First Edition

Library of Congress Cataloging-in-Publication Data

Yolen, Jane.
 The girl in the golden bower / written by Jane Yolen ; illustrated by Jane
Dyer. — 1st ed.
  p. cm.
 Summary: After the death of her parents, a young girl is left at
the mercy of a sorceress who thinks the girl can help her get a
treasure.
ISBN 0-316-96894-3 (hc)   ISBN 0-316-96939-7 (pb)
 [1. Fairy tales. 2. Magic — Fiction.] I. Dyer, Jane, ill.
II. Title.
PZ8.Y78Ge   1994
[E] — dc20   92-37284
          HC: 10 9 8 7 6 5 4 3 2
          PB: 10 9 8 7 6 5 4 3 2 1

          NIL

Published simultaneously in Canada
by Little, Brown & Company (Canada) Limited

Illustrations done in Winsor and Newton watercolors
on Waterford 140-pound hot press paper
Color separations made by New Interlitho
Text set in Goudy by Typographic House

Printed and bound by New Interlitho

Printed in Italy

For Christine Crow, who has entertained me in her
St. Andrews bower, with love — J. Y.

For Brookie, with the
golden hair — J. D.

Once in a stone house on the edge of a tangled forest lived a woodsman. He had been born in that house, as had his father before him. They each, in their turn, served the royal family whose castle lay deep in the wood.

But after the queen's untimely death, the king disappeared on a hunt, and his bowmen with him. The servants eventually departed. The castle became overgrown with briars; thistle and thorn crept through the cracks in the courtyard, and woodbine twined along the stairs. No one lived in the castle now, except the little animals who scratched and scrabbled in the undergrowth and — so the tales went — one great beast.

The beast had a head like a lion's, with a golden mane as tangled as the woods. It had the body of a deer and feet of horn. Its tail was as sinuous as a serpent's, its eyes as sharp as a hawk's. And its roar was like thunder between the hills.

For many years the woodsman lived alone in the stone house. But one day, soon after the king disappeared, the woodsman found a frail young woman wandering along the forest's edge. There was something permanently lost about her, as if everything she had in the world was gone, even her name. She owned nothing but the dress she wore, made with tiny stitches both neat and fair, and a plain comb the color of her long russet hair.

The woodsman took her in. He fed her and clothed her, and in time the two of them fell deeply in love. They married there, in the tangled wood, and when the young woman gave birth to a yellow-haired child, they called her Aurea, which means gold.

Now, one day, when Aurea was five, another woman came to the woodsman's house. This one was dressed all in green, with woods-green eyes and the manners of a cat. She was willing to cook in exchange for a room and a bed, but she was no ordinary cook. She was a sorceress, the daughter of a sorcerer, who had come to the woods seeking a great treasure. She was certain that a charm leading to the treasure lay in the woodsman's domain, and she was determined to find it. Since the woodsman's wife was frail, they asked the cook to bide with them.

For Aurea, whose worth she discounted, the sorceress cooked nothing but cottage porridge, with much water and a quick turn of the spoon. But for the woodsman and his wife, she made excellent vernal pottages of wild-horse parsley and omelettes with clary and cream. She baked puddings of garden patience and boiled chamomile tea. She cooked delicious meals, for she meant to be kept on as long as she needed to search for the charm.

"Her meals are fit for the king," said the woodsman.

At his words, his wife looked lost again, but the green-eyed sorceress only smiled.

One soft day in spring, the cook made a mushroom stew for the woodsman and his wife and a bowl of cottage porridge for the child. But some of the mushrooms must have been bad, for the wife took deathly ill. She called Aurea to her bedside and, handing her the russet comb, said, "It is all I can leave you, my child, all that is mine alone to give. It belonged to my mother, who gave it to me. It will watch over you when I cannot." And so saying, she died.

"I shall keep it always," Aurea whispered, putting the comb into her own hair.

The comb shimmered for a moment, then turned from brown to gold. It was impossible to tell where Aurea's hair ended and the comb began, so perfectly did the colors match.

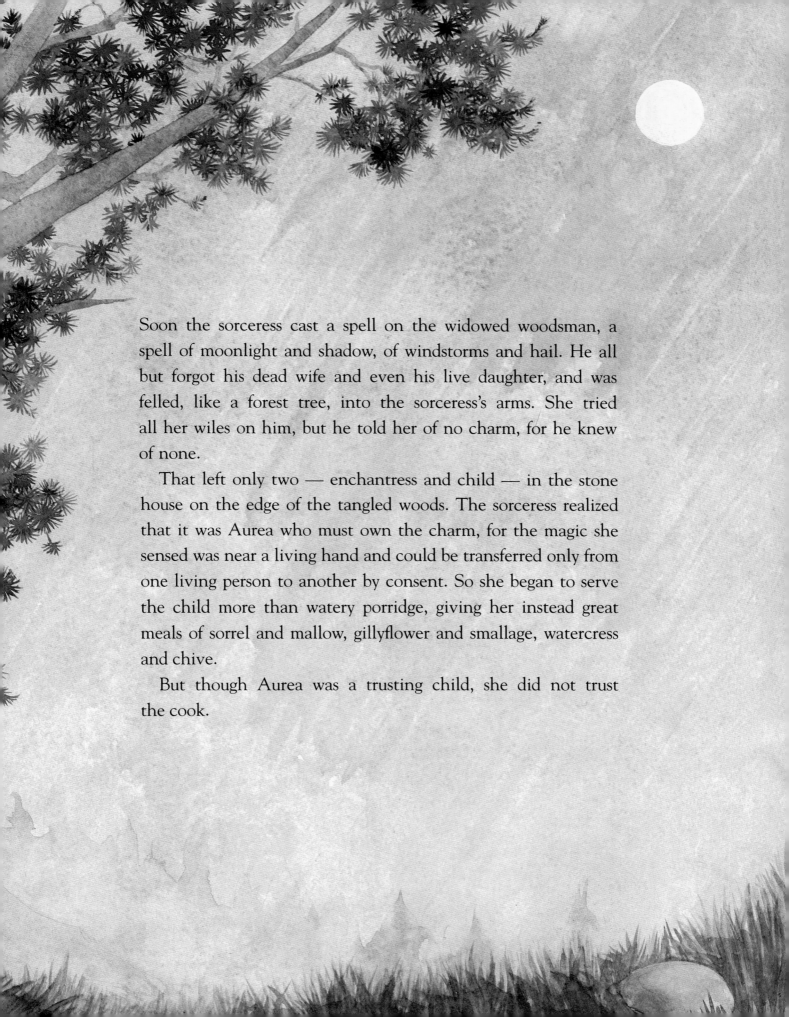

Soon the sorceress cast a spell on the widowed woodsman, a spell of moonlight and shadow, of windstorms and hail. He all but forgot his dead wife and even his live daughter, and was felled, like a forest tree, into the sorceress's arms. She tried all her wiles on him, but he told her of no charm, for he knew of none.

That left only two — enchantress and child — in the stone house on the edge of the tangled woods. The sorceress realized that it was Aurea who must own the charm, for the magic she sensed was near a living hand and could be transferred only from one living person to another by consent. So she began to serve the child more than watery porridge, giving her instead great meals of sorrel and mallow, gillyflower and smallage, watercress and chive.

But though Aurea was a trusting child, she did not trust the cook.

She turned instead to the forest animals, who came trustingly to her, by ones and twos and threes: the rabbit and ferret; the otter and squirrel; the field mouse and muskrat; the marten, fox, and lynx. She fed them and sang to them and entrusted her secrets to their ears alone. And when they became tame enough to settle by her side, she took the golden comb from her hair and curried the tangles from their fur, singing:

> *Tangle, twist, snarl, and knot;*
> *I take from you what has been caught.*

Then she loosed the thistles and briars and burrs from their fur into the wind.

Next she braided strands of her own golden hair into theirs, singing:

> *Tangle, knot, twist, and twine;*
> *I give to you what once was mine.*

Soon the woods around the stone house were full of these half-tame creatures with fur fantastically twined and braided with gold.

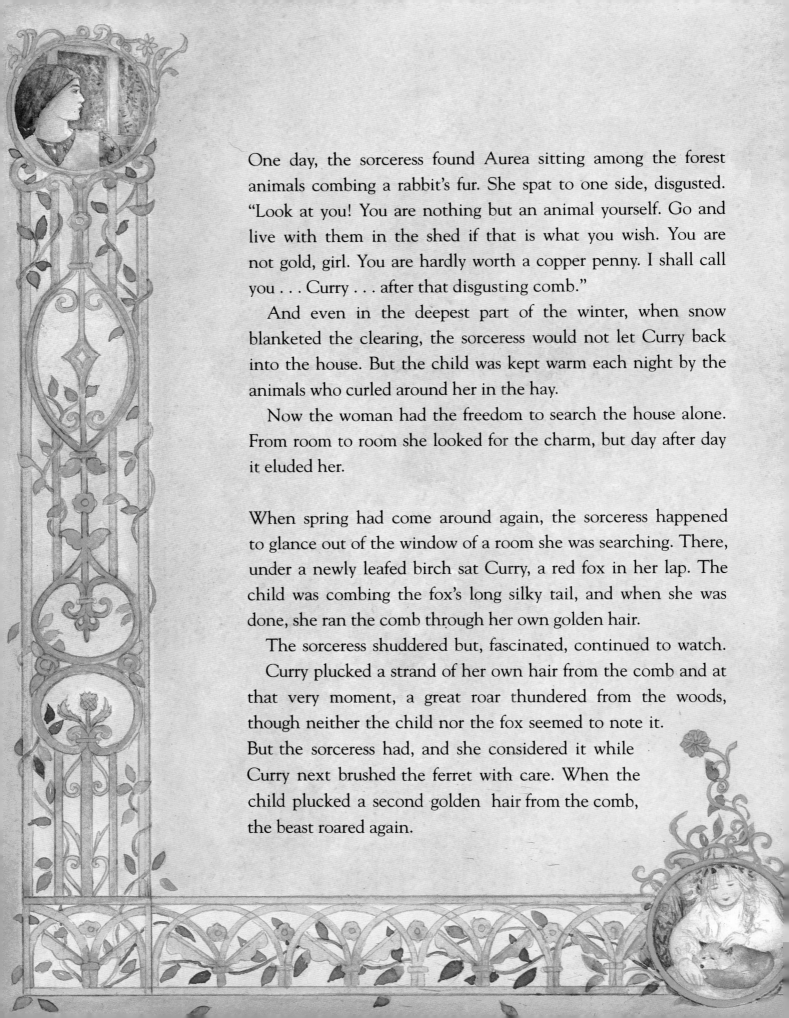

One day, the sorceress found Aurea sitting among the forest animals combing a rabbit's fur. She spat to one side, disgusted. "Look at you! You are nothing but an animal yourself. Go and live with them in the shed if that is what you wish. You are not gold, girl. You are hardly worth a copper penny. I shall call you . . . Curry . . . after that disgusting comb."

And even in the deepest part of the winter, when snow blanketed the clearing, the sorceress would not let Curry back into the house. But the child was kept warm each night by the animals who curled around her in the hay.

Now the woman had the freedom to search the house alone. From room to room she looked for the charm, but day after day it eluded her.

When spring had come around again, the sorceress happened to glance out of the window of a room she was searching. There, under a newly leafed birch sat Curry, a red fox in her lap. The child was combing the fox's long silky tail, and when she was done, she ran the comb through her own golden hair.

The sorceress shuddered but, fascinated, continued to watch.

Curry plucked a strand of her own hair from the comb and at that very moment, a great roar thundered from the woods, though neither the child nor the fox seemed to note it. But the sorceress had, and she considered it while Curry next brushed the ferret with care. When the child plucked a second golden hair from the comb, the beast roared again.

The sorceress knew then that her search was done. Running outside, she called with a voice sweetened as with honey: "Child . . . Curry . . . Aurea . . . let me borrow your comb."

But Curry was not fooled by the woman's tone. So, forgetting for a moment that consent was needed, the sorceress tried to snatch away the comb. It turned first red hot, then white, and left the mark of its teeth in her palm. She dropped the comb and put her hand to her mouth, as if her breath might salve the pain.

"That was my mother's comb," said Curry. "You shall not have it." She picked the comb up and put it back into her hair. For a moment — just a moment — it shimmered. Then it turned to gold, and no one could tell where the hair ended and the comb began.

Furious with humiliation and pain, the sorceress grabbed Curry by the hair. Despite the child's cries, she yanked her to her feet and dragged her deep and deeper into the dark woods. At last, many miles away, they came to a clearing, marked by red and white roses.

Curry wept and begged to go back, but the sorceress held her fast till, worn out by weeping, the child fell asleep. Only then did the sorceress let her go, casting a spell to deepen Curry's natural sleep:

> *Roses red and roses white,*
> *Turn her day to deepest night.*

She added to herself: "In a week she shall be dead of starvation, and I shall return to claim the comb from her bones."

Curry slept on and on, through the day and into the night. As she slept, the wind gathered the thistles and burrs she had curried from the animals' fur and blew them into the deep woods, building her a tidy nest. As she slept even longer, her wild friends crept around her: the rabbit and ferret; the otter and squirrel; the field mouse and muskrat; the marten, fox, and lynx. One by one by one, they took the comb and ran it through her golden hair. The more they combed, the longer her hair grew, till it twined about her in an intricate bower and covered her over with a golden cloth. Lullabied by her animal friends, Curry slept on and on, and in her sleep grew from a child into a girl, from a girl into a lovely young woman.

And the animals, satisfied, crept away.

But the sorceress did not know this. Back in the stone house, she made her plans, reciting them aloud for comfort. She waited a full week before daring to go out again into the woods. Then, taking shears to cut the comb from the dead child's hair, she followed the long path back.

When she came to the clearing where red and white roses should have marked the site, there was only gold. A golden gate, high as a door, stood across the path. Golden webbings wound in and out of the bushes. Every rose had petals patined in gold; every leaf and thorn was outlined in it, making the clearing into an intricate golden cage.

Carefully the sorceress lifted the latch, pushed open the gate, and peered in. There was no sign of the child Curry, but on a couch of pure gold lay the most beautiful young woman she had ever seen, at least a princess, most probably a queen.

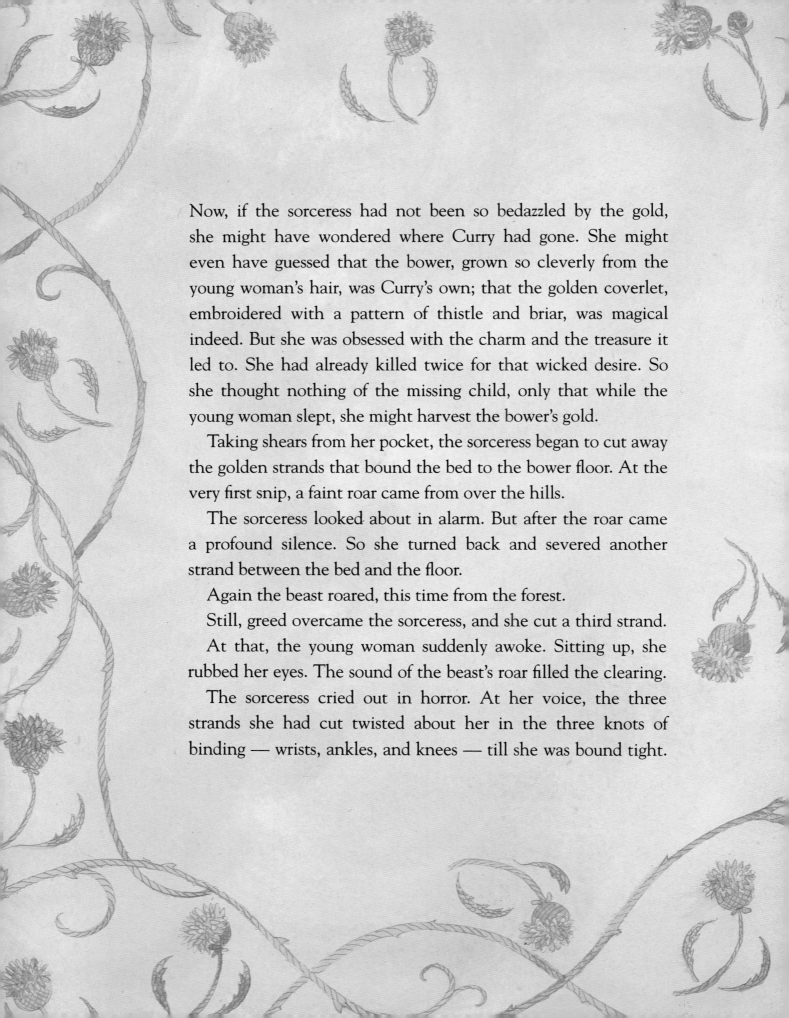

Now, if the sorceress had not been so bedazzled by the gold, she might have wondered where Curry had gone. She might even have guessed that the bower, grown so cleverly from the young woman's hair, was Curry's own; that the golden coverlet, embroidered with a pattern of thistle and briar, was magical indeed. But she was obsessed with the charm and the treasure it led to. She had already killed twice for that wicked desire. So she thought nothing of the missing child, only that while the young woman slept, she might harvest the bower's gold.

Taking shears from her pocket, the sorceress began to cut away the golden strands that bound the bed to the bower floor. At the very first snip, a faint roar came from over the hills.

The sorceress looked about in alarm. But after the roar came a profound silence. So she turned back and severed another strand between the bed and the floor.

Again the beast roared, this time from the forest.

Still, greed overcame the sorceress, and she cut a third strand.

At that, the young woman suddenly awoke. Sitting up, she rubbed her eyes. The sound of the beast's roar filled the clearing.

The sorceress cried out in horror. At her voice, the three strands she had cut twisted about her in the three knots of binding — wrists, ankles, and knees — till she was bound tight.

The young woman threw off the gold coverlet and stood, her long golden hair shorn to the waist. Going to the golden gate, she called:

> *Tangle, twist, snarl, and knot;*
> *I take from you what has been caught.*

"Do not open the gate," the sorceress cried, "or the beast will come in and devour us."

But the young woman pushed open the door.

All the little creatures of the forest crowded in as if they, too, were afraid: the rabbit and ferret; the otter and squirrel; the field mouse and muskrat; the marten, fox, and lynx. Only once they passed through the golden gate, they were no longer *little* creatures at all, for they grew tall, taller, and taller still, till they were handsome men, each carrying a hunting bow.

Just as the last came through the gate, there was an over-powering roar, and there, in the clearing, was the great beast itself.

"Close the gate," cried the sorceress. "Bowmen, aim well."

But the bowmen did not even nock their arrows, and the young woman did not close the gate. Instead she walked through it, toward the beast.

The beast roared again, showing a hundred sharp teeth.

Minding neither teeth nor roar, the young woman smiled. Taking a golden comb from her hair, she began to comb the beast's tangled mane, saying:

Tangle, knot, twist, and twine;
I give to you what once was mine.

The beast closed its terrible mouth and submitted quietly to the comb. When the last bit of its mane was smooth, the maiden took strands of her own golden hair and braided it into the beast's forelock. Then, pulling gently on the braid, she led the beast into the bower.

This time the sorceress was silent. As maiden and beast passed through the gate, the beast grew tall and taller and taller still, until he was a stately, brown-haired man with a gold medallion like a rose in his hat. At the same time, the young woman grew small and smaller and smaller still, until she was once again a little girl named Aurea in a tattered dress.

The tall man knelt before her in wonder. "I was called to the bower by the power of a charm my wife once owned. I followed you in because you looked like my daughter, save for the color of your hair. But she was a princess, and now I see you are but a tattered child."

"I am not your daughter, sir," said Aurea. "My father was a woodsman, not a king. And the only gold he owned was in my hair."

"My daughter was more precious to me than gold," said the king. "She was my treasure. When my wife died and my daughter was lost in the woods through a sorcerer's wiles, I went mad with grief. My kingdom sank into ruin while I sought my daughter, till at last I was changed by the sorcerer's magic into a wild and ravenous beast."

Aurea looked at him strangely. "Did your daughter have hair the same color as yours?"

"Yes, child, and a comb to match it. A magic comb given to her by her mother to keep her safe, for all the good it did."

"Then I am your daughter's daughter," she said. "For here, Grandfather, is that very comb." She handed it to him, and as it passed from her hand to his, it shimmered for a moment. Just a moment. Then it turned from gold to brown.

The king picked up his little granddaughter then, placing her upon his shoulders. In this manner, with the bowmen behind them, they made their way back to the ruined castle.

But when they got there, they found the castle was in ruins no more. Briars had been changed to red roses, woodbine to white.

What a welcome they made themselves: music and feasting for seven days and seven nights, till they were all quite tired of it. And after, they lived happily for the rest of their lives.

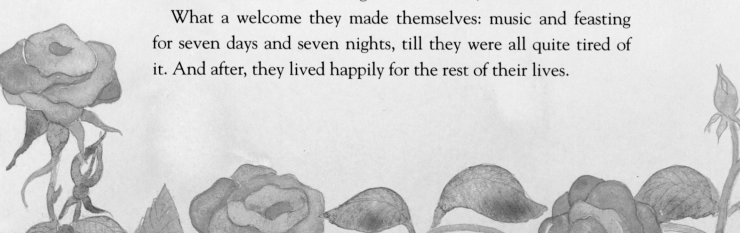

As for the sorceress, her ending was quite different. If you go from the stone house down a winding path deep, then deeper, and deeper still into the woods, you will come across a clearing marked out by red roses and white. In the center of that clearing is a cage of green boughs in which sits a green-eyed bird. The bird is fed daily by the king's new woodsman on a diet of sorrel and mallow, gillyflower and smallage, watercress and chive. But though the door of the cage stands open, the bird does not leave. It is held to that spot by fear, though there is nothing in the woods to be afraid of. And it is kept in the cage by strong bars of gold, though there are none to be seen. Except in its heart.

Except in its heart.